E   Watanabe, Shigeo, *97*
WAT   1928-

        Ice cream is
        falling

    $10.95

DATE			

books by
Shigeo Watanabe and Yasuo Ohtomo

I Love Special Days books
It's My Birthday!

I Can Do It All By Myself books
How do I put it on?
An American Library Association
Notable Children's Book

What a good lunch!

Get set! Go!

I'm king of the castle!

I can ride it!

Where's my daddy?

I can build a house!

I can take a walk!

I Love To Do Things With Daddy books
Daddy, play with me!
I can take a bath!

American text copyright © 1989 by Philomel Books, a division of The Putnam & Grosset Group,
200 Madison Avenue, New York, NY 10016. Published simultaneously in Canada. Text copyright
© 1979 by Shigeo Watanabe. Illustrations copyright © 1979 by Yasuo Ohtomo. Originally published by Akane Shobo, Tokyo, Japan, under the title: *Aisukuriimu Ga Futtekita.* American translation rights arranged with Akane Shobo Co., Ltd., through Japan Foreign Rights Centre. Printed in
Hong Kong by Wing King Tong, Co., Ltd. All rights reserved.

Library of Congress Cataloging-in-Publication Data   Watanabe, Shigeo, 1928–   [Aisukuriimu Ga
Futtekita. English]   Ice cream is falling / Shigeo Watanabe; pictures by Yasuo Ohtomo.
p.   cm.   Translation of: Aisukuriimu Ga Futtekita. Summary: Bear and his friends have a wonder-
ful time playing when they see snow for the first time.   ISBN 0-399-21550-6   [1. Bears—Fiction.
2. Snow—Fiction.] I. Ōtomo, Yasuo, ill. II. Title. PZ7.W2615Ig   1989 E—dc19   88-38299 CIP AC
First impression

Ice Cream Is Falling!

Shigeo Watanabe   Pictures by Yasuo Ohtomo

Philomel Books   New York

Bear opened his eyes. He sat up and listened as hard as
he could. There was something different this morning.
He couldn't hear the hum of cars passing on the street.

He couldn't hear the loud noises of the garbage truck. Through a crack in his curtains, Bear could see that it was very bright outside.

Everything he saw was white. The bushes were white, the trees were white, and his tricycle was just a white lump on the lawn.

Bear rushed to wake up his mother.
"Mommy, Mommy, come and see!"
His mother got up and opened her curtains.
"Goodness, Bear, it's snowing!" she said.
"Like ice cream falling from the sky," Bear sang out.
He was so excited that he ran out of the house
and into the snow in his pajamas.

Bear walked all over the deep drifts on the lawn.
Crunch, crunch, his feet sank down into the white snow.
"Ooh," he gasped. "It's cold."
Bear scooped up some snow from the ground
and tasted it.
"Ooh, it *is* cold!"
Snowflakes fell on his head and neck. He was freezing!
Bear ran inside, leaving one, two, three, four, five, six
footprints behind in the snowy yard.

There had not been snow in Bear's town for years.
Now the buses had stopped running. There were no cars
on the road. There were no deliveries being made.

Before long, Bear's friends came outside to play.
"Everything's white!" cried Fox and Rabbit as they came
running through the snow.
"You are too!" Raccoon said.

"It's snowing, it's snowing!" shouted Dog. He rolled
over in the fresh snow.

"I want to go outside, too!" Bear told his mother. So she helped him dress in his sweater, warm woolly jacket, winter hat and boots.

"Whee!" Bear shouted. But as he rushed out, he slipped in the snow. "At least I'm here," Bear laughed.

Bear guessed what would happen next. Fox picked up
some snow and packed it into a fluffy snowball.

"Watch out!" Bear called.

Rabbit threw a snowball back. Soon there was a big snowball fight. Snowballs whizzed through the air and snow flew everywhere.

"Snow only looks soft!" Dog said.
"I've got an idea," said Bear. "Let's build
a snowman!"

Everyone helped gather the cold snow and shape it into a large ball.

The ball grew and grew until it looked like a round
mountain.

It was the body of a gigantic snowman.

Fox and Rabbit rolled more snow into a large snowball.
They rolled it and rolled it.

It was the snowman's head.
"Careful," Bear said, as they all helped put it on
the giant body.

"He has no eyes," Dog said. Raccoon brought two tangerines.
"He needs ears, too," said Rabbit, and he found some
leaves. Fox put a twig in the snowman for a mouth.

"All he needs now is a hat," Fox said. Hog found a fine
hat that looked just right.

"He's finished!" Bear and his friends yelled and clapped
their hands.

"Am I as tall as Snowman?" Bear asked.
"Almost," Rabbit said.

When Daddy came home that starry night, the snowman
was standing alone in the road.
"Goodnight, Snowman," he said.

And Bear dreamed of his snowy day.